KING KUSHA

SHEELAVATI, THE CHIEF QUEEN OF THE HEIRLESS KING OKKAKA OF KUSHAVATI, WAS OFFERED A BOON BY INDRA, KING OF THE GODS.

YOU SHALL HAVE TWO SONS. ONE WISE BUT UGLY, THE OTHER HANDSOME BUT A FOOL. WHICH WILL YOU HAVE FIRST?

THE WISE ONE, MY LORD.

IN DUE COURSE, SHEELAVATI GAVE BIRTH TO A SON.

HE SHALL BE CALLED KUSHA.

WHEN THEY REACHED SAGALA, THEY WERE RECEIVED GRACIOUSLY BY THE KING, THE QUEEN, PRINCESS PRABHAVATI AND HER SEVEN YOUNGER SISTERS.

LATER, WHEN PRABHAVATI CAME TO PAY HER RESPECTS TO SHEELAVATI —

SHOULD THIS DAZZLING BEAUTY SEE MY SON'S FACE, SHE WILL RUN AWAY FROM HIM THAT VERY MOMENT. YET I MUST NOT FAIL MY SON. LET ME SEE WHAT I CAN DO.

WHEN PRABHAVATI HAD LEFT, SHEELAVATI SPOKE TO THE KING OF MADDA.

YOUR DAUGHTER IS WORTHY OF MY SON. BUT...

YES?

PRABHAVATI AGREED TO RESPECT THE TRADITION AND AFTER MUCH GIVING AND RECEIVING OF GIFTS, OKKAKA AND SHEELAVATI ESCORTED THEIR DAUGHTER-IN-LAW, ALONG WITH HER NURSE AND A VAST RETINUE, TO KUSHAVATI.

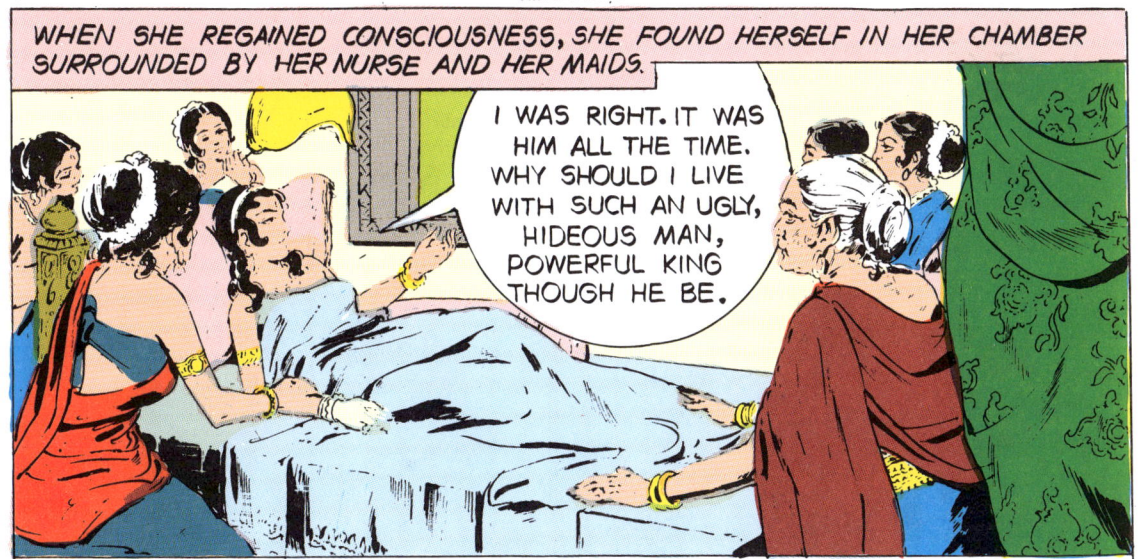

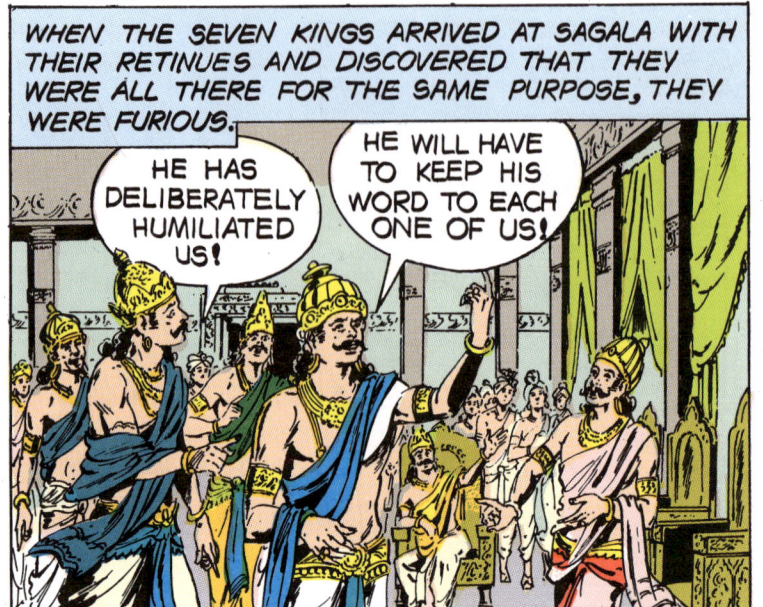

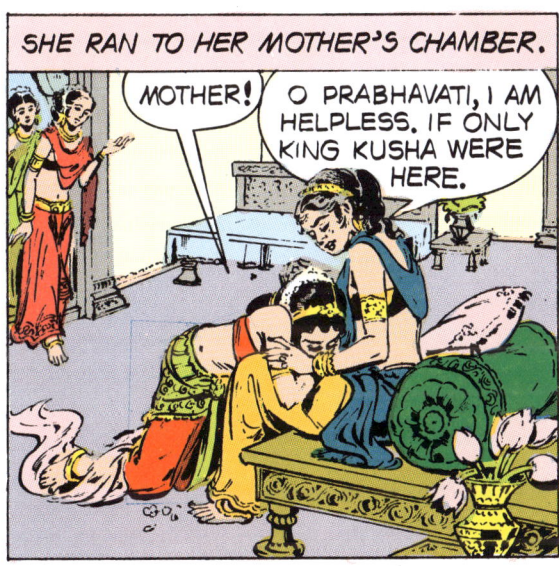

KUSHA SETTLED MATTERS BY OFFERING HIS SEVEN SISTERS-IN-LAW TO THE SEVEN KINGS.

THEN HE AND PRABHAVATI WENT TO KUSHAVATI WHERE THEY LIVED HAPPILY EVER AFTER.

9 amazing offers on your favourite reads!

1
Get additional 20% off on ACK Complete Collection.
Code: ACKCC20
www.amarchitrakatha.com

2
Get additional 15% off on any ACK Complete Collection Volumes (1, 2 & 3).
Code: ACKV15
www.amarchitrakatha.com

3
Get flat 15% off on all India Book House books on amarchitrakatha.com.
Code: IBHACK15
www.amarchitrakatha.com

4
Get additional 20% off on 1 year Subscription of Tinkle magazine
Code: TINKLE20
www.amarchitrakatha.com

5
Get additional 25% off on 1 year Subscription of Tinkle Combo
Code: ACKTC25
www.amarchitrakatha.com

6
Get additional 10% off on 1 year Subscription of Brainwave
Code: BRAINWAVE10
www.amarchitrakatha.com

7
Get flat 30% discount on all Karadi Products on Amarchitrakatha.com.
Code: KARADI30
www.amarchitrakatha.com

8
Get additional 15% off on 1 year Subscription of Nationa Geographic
Code: NATGEO15
getnationalgeographic.com

9
Get additional 5% off on 1 year Subscription of National Geographic Magazine and National Geographic Traveller India Combo
Code: NGC05
getnationalgeographic.com

How to Redeem:
1. Log on to www.amarchitrakatha.com for Amar Chitra Katha offers and www.getnationalgeographic.com for National Geographic offers
2. Select the products you wish to buy and add to your shopping cart.
3. Proceed to "Checkout & Pay" and enter the coupon code in discount Code section. Click on the "Verify" button & proceed with the address and payments details.

Terms and Conditions:
1. Customers can redeem the coupon code only at our online stores.
2. To avail the discount, customer will have to submit the coupon code at the checkout page.
3. ACK Media reserves the right to change or withdraw the offer and/or the promo codes, anytime, at the sole discretion of the management.
4. All standard Terms & Conditions available at amarchitrakatha.com & getnationalgeographic.com will apply.

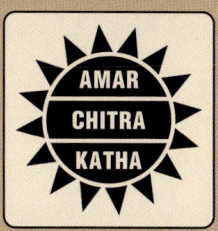

VASAVADATTA
THE PRINCESS WHO CAPTIVATED A TRUE KSHATRIYA

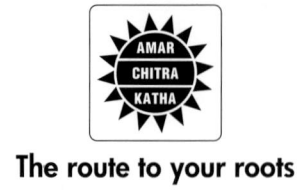

The route to your roots

VASAVADATTA

King Udayana may have been imprisoned, but his mind roamed free. Udayana could charm even the beasts of the forest with his music. Vasavadatta, the beautiful daughter of his captor, inspired him to escape the shackles of his enemy. An example of kshatriya honour and passion, their romance has been described by Indian poets and bards since ancient times.

Script
Meena Talim

Illustrations
Pratap Mulick

Editor
Anant Pai

This Amar Chitra Katha is based on the Dhamma-pada-atthakatha (5th century AD).

> ONE DAY, AS HE WAS RETURNING FROM HIS GARDEN –

"MINISTER, IS THERE A KING WHO IS GREATER THAN I AM?"

"EXCUSE ME, YOUR MAJESTY! THERE IS ONE SUCH KING."

"WHO IS IT?"

"KING UDAYANA OF KAUSHAMBI."

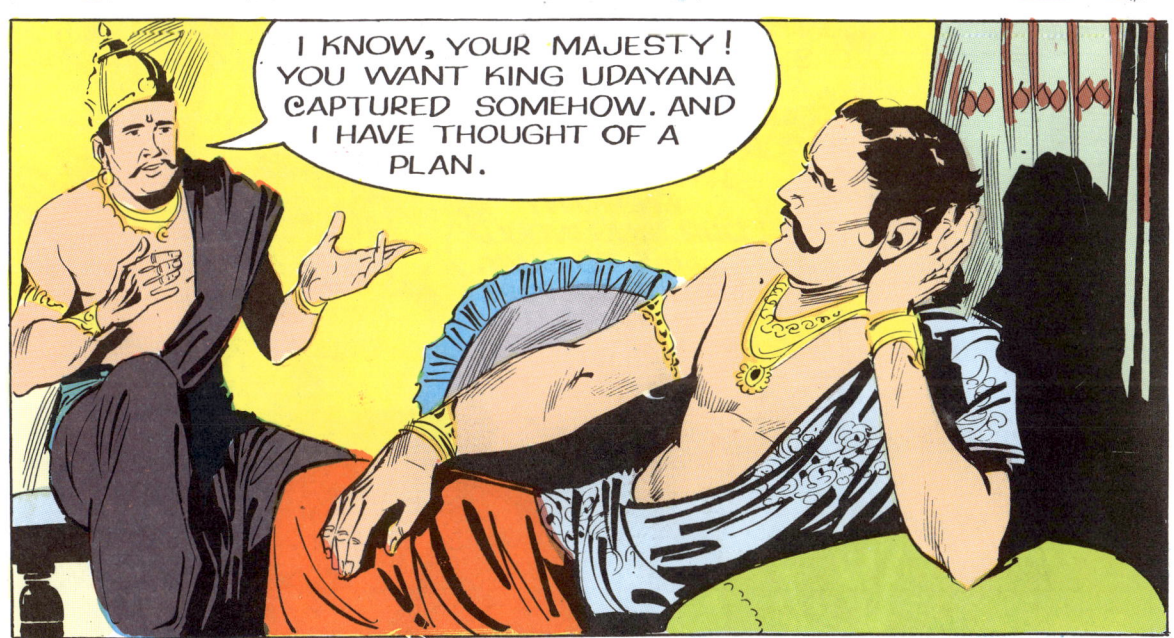

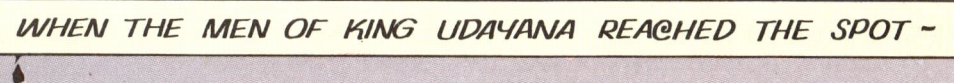

A STOCKADE WAS BUILT OUTSIDE UJJAINI AND THE MINISTER SENT MEN TO OBTAIN NEWS OF KING UDAYANA.

UDAYANA, MEANWHILE WAS HELD CAPTIVE IN PRADYOTA'S KINGDOM.

GUARD! I HAVE BEEN HERE FOR THREE DAYS. WHEN DO I SEE YOUR KING?

I DON'T KNOW. HIS MAJESTY HAS BEEN BUSY CELEBRATING HIS VICTORY OVER YOU.

UDAYANA LIFTED THE FRINGE OF THE CURTAIN...

...AND WAS ASTONISHED TO SEE THE BEAUTIFUL PRINCESS.

WHO ARE YOU?

I AM VASAVADATTA, DAUGHTER OF KING PRADYOTA. AND YOU?

"CAN I BE OF ANY HELP?"

"YOUR FATHER WILL DO ANYTHING TO HELP YOU MASTER THE CHANT."

"...TELL HIM, YOU NEED AN ELEPHANT TO PUT YOUR KNOWLEDGE TO TEST."

"I'LL DO THAT."

THE KING READILY ACCEDED TO HIS DAUGHTER'S REQUEST AND AN ELEPHANT WAS PLACED AT HER DISPOSAL.

BUT WHEN KING PRADYOTA HEARD THE STRANGE REQUEST...

I THINK, THIS MUST BE A RUSE WORKED OUT BY UDAYANA TO ESCAPE FROM HERE.

VERY WELL, A GATE WILL BE LEFT OPEN.

THANK YOU, FATHER.

THE KING CALLED FOR HIS SPIES.

LISTEN CAREFULLY. DON'T LET KING UDAYANA KNOW THAT HE IS BEING FOLLOWED. CAPTURE HIM ONLY IF HE TRIES TO RUN AWAY.

AS YOU WISH, YOUR MAJESTY.

BY THEN KING UDAYANA HAD REACHED THE BORDERS OF UJJAINI.

IT IS OUR KING! LET US RUSH TO HIS HELP.

UDAYANA'S MINISTER WHO HAD BEEN IN TOUCH WITH HIM ALL THESE DAYS, WAS THERE TO RECEIVE HIM.

THE TIRED AND EXHAUSTED SOLDIERS OF KING PRADYOTA WERE EASILY OVERPOWERED BY KING UDAYANA'S MEN.

BACK IN KAUSHAMBI, KING UDAYANA WAS GIVEN A WARM WELCOME BY HIS PEOPLE.

PRINCESS VASAVADATTA WAS MARRIED TO HIM AMIDST GREAT REJOICING.

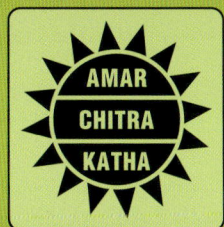

THE ACROBAT

A COLLECTION OF BUDDHIST TALES

The route to your roots

THE ACROBAT

A talented acrobat, a hard-working farmer, a love-lorn youth and a distraught mother all have something in common. Their lives are affected by Gautam Buddha. He comes to each one of them when the time is right and touches their hearts and minds in such a way that their troubles cease to exist and they are completely at peace.

Script	Illustrations	Editor
Gayatri Madan Dutt	Dilip Kadam	Anant Pai

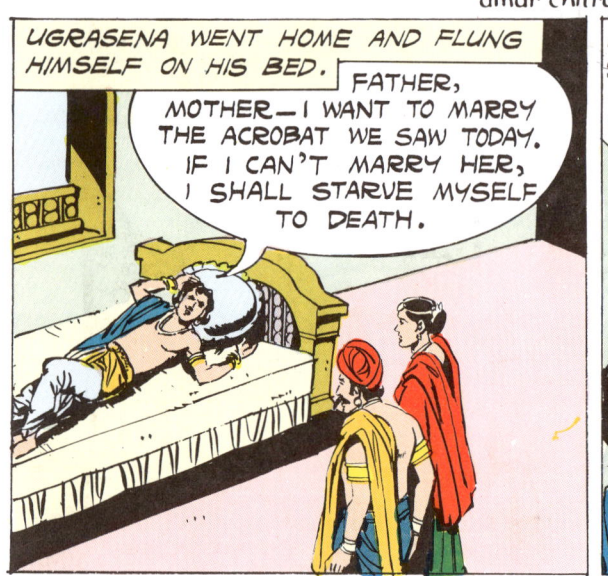

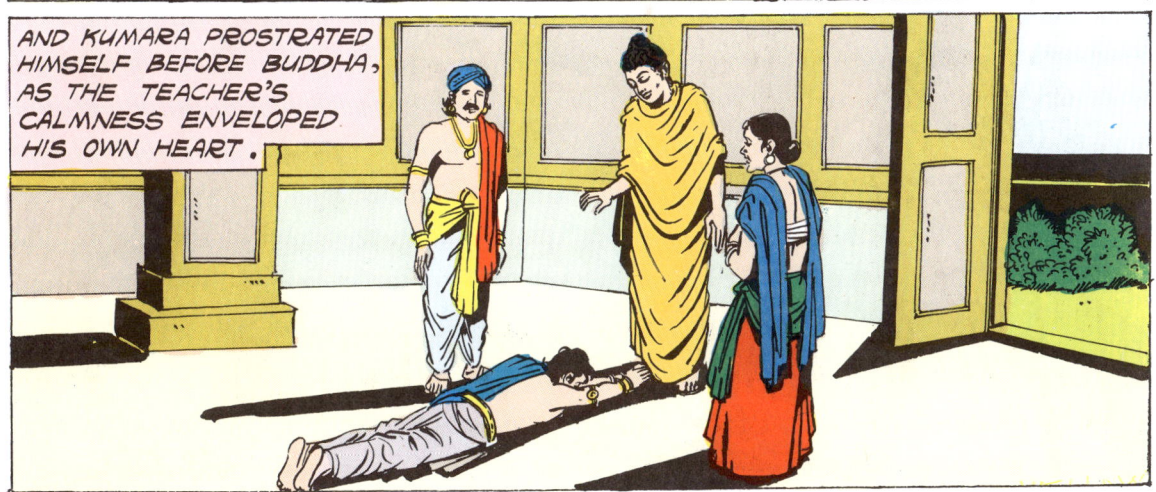

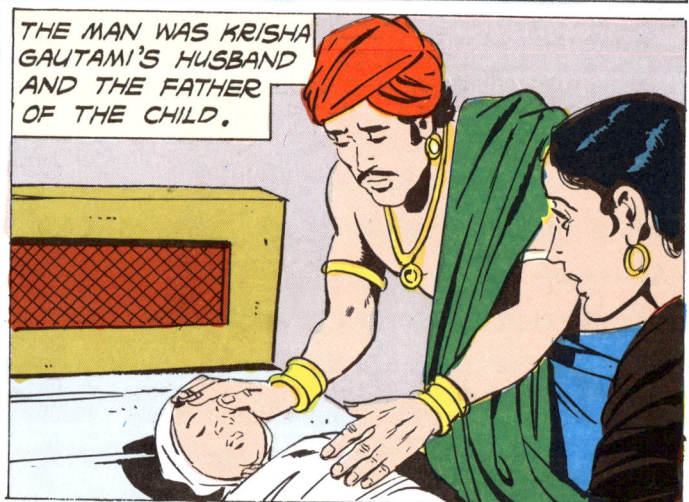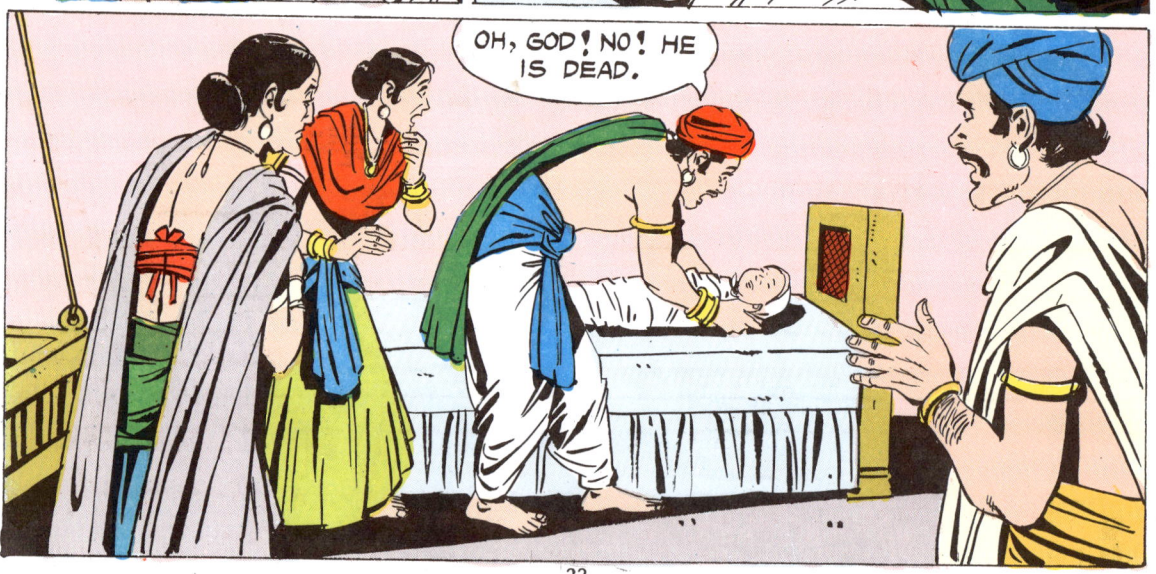

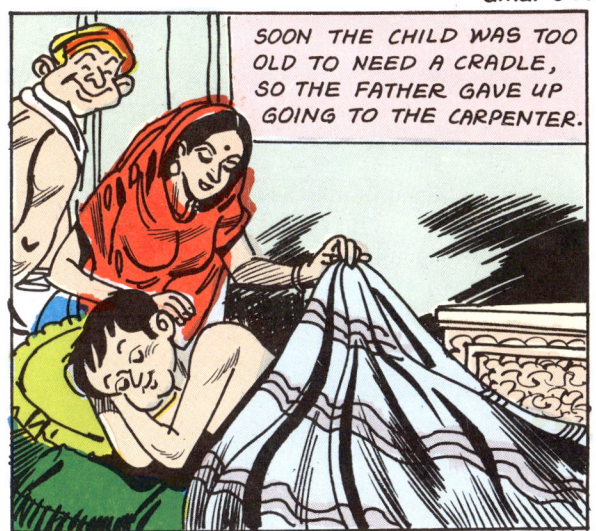

SUBSCRIBE NOW!

Additional 10% OFF on purchase from www.amarchitrakatha.com
Coupon Code: ACKTINKLE10

TINKLE COMBO
MAGAZINE + DIGEST
1 year subscription

Pay only ₹1200 **₹880!**

FREE
2 Time Compass DVDs worth ₹598

TINKLE MAGAZINE
1 year subscription

Pay only ₹480 **₹380!**

I would like a one year subscription for
TINKLE COMBO ☐ **TINKLE MAGAZINE** ☐
(Please tick the appropriate box)

YOUR DETAILS*

Name: .... Date of Birth: |__|__| / |__|__| / |__|__|__|__|

Address: ....

.... City: .... Pin: |__|__|__|__|__|__| State: ....

School: .... Class: ....

Tel: .... Mobile: + 91 - |__|__|__|__|__|__|__|__|__|__|

Email: .... Signature: ....

PAYMENT OPTIONS

☐ Cheque /DD:

Please find enclosed Cheque /DD no. |__|__|__|__|__|__| drawn in favour of 'ACK Media Direct Pvt. Ltd.'

at .... (bank) for the amount ....,

dated |__|__| / |__|__| / |__|__|__|__| and send it to: IBH Books & Magazines Distributers Pvt. Ltd., Arch No. 30, West Approach, Below Mahalaxmi Bridge, Mahalaxmi (W), Mumbai - 400034.

☐ Pay Cash on Delivery: Pay cash on delivery of the first issue to the postman. (Additional charge of ₹50 applicable)

☐ Pay by money order: Pay by money order in favour of "ACK Media Direct Pvt. Ltd."

☐ Online subscription: Please visit: www.amarchitrakatha.com

For any queries or further information: Email: customerservice@ack-media.com or Call: 022-40497435 / 36